When the **EARTH** was Quiet

When the EARTH was Quiet

GABRIEL ANTHONY LOPEZ

When the Earth was Quiet

Printed in the United States of America
ISBN 978-1-64133-797-7 (hc)
ISBN 978-1-64133-792-2 (sc)
ISBN 978-1-64133-793-9 (ebk)

2024.03.06

BlueInk Media Solutions
1111B S Governors Ave
STE 7582 Dover,
DE 19904

www.blueinkmediasolutions.com

Table of Contents

CHAPTER I

Ghost dances are everywhere. The silence of the earth is there. Lydia Miller grabbed a shovel and dove into the sediment of the Badlands of Montana. She was crouched alone on some land next to an outcrop. The sun was setting, and the major stars were starting to twinkle in the sky. Lydia kept digging until the water from the bucket was mostly dirty. She had finished another day of hard work. Taking her hat off and feeling the cool breeze of autumn she walked over to her tent. Some of the trees glistened in their golden hue against the sunset. She looked through her papers on a makeshift desk. She sat there for a while and what she wrote continued to astound even her. She placed some remaining palaeontologic and geologic samples in one of the newest scientific instruments.

She waited for the results. The readings from the instrument confirmed her astonishment. It is the year 2240 and humanity has made great scientific advancements. She looked at a model of a *Parasaurolophus*. Next to it was one of a *Velociraptor*. *Predator and prey, she thought.*

The lights flickered on and off in Lydia's tent. She still wondered what it all meant and if it was all worth it. This was her life's work. *If only she could go further with it,* she thought. The world she was discovering had proven beneficial to humanity, but what she finally wrote now was either doom or hope.

CHAPTER II

Max Rodriguez gazed out over the verdant green canopies of the Cascades. His house was remote, but not remote enough for his nature-loving side. He thought of Lydia who was currently in Montana. She had always taken a more brazen way to her work, making deadlines, and using the latest in everything. *I wonder what she was doing*, he thought. He looked at some of his recent bone specimen samples on his desk. One had *Wadhi al Hitan* written on it. It came from the Sahara Desert in Egypt. Being in Egypt was thrilling. He got to use some of his archaeological skills. When they went further into Africa on the west coast, he used some of his anthropological skills with some native tribes. Max had been on many research expeditions lately. Some nights in Africa he would look up to the stars. Sometimes he forgot humanity was already living among the stars. Paleontology, geology, and anthropology were only among a few of his interests. He enjoyed paleobiology and cosmology like Lydia.

He went into the kitchen for a cup of coffee. The rich aroma tantalized his senses. He found a memory book of photos. The gazes of his parents were captured well in the photos. *They were taken from him*, he thought. That fateful night continues to haunt him to this day. Looking along his wall he studied his album of photographs from around the world—Mexico, India, China, Turkey, and Ethiopia. Further down the wall were some complete dinosaur skeletons of small theropod dinosaurs. The trees outside whipped into a frenzy as the wind blew against his home. He looked at the weather. A small storm was approaching. *Would they come back?* he thought.

He had always taken to the assumption that the theories dealing with the dinosaurs were not so one-directional. All lead to extinction. He was about life although he continually fought death in the back of his mind. The eerie sounds of gunfire replayed again, over and over.

Thinking of Lydia did not do him any good as of late. And, thinking of all the people on his crew even less. The scientific work was becoming remote to him, and he forced himself to focus on it. He threw some papers across the room. *If only they had not died*, Max thought. He was young then when his parents died—he was eleven or so. Now, at thirty-two he thought he would have more direction. The virus that took his mother and father was a lethal one. Max knew better than to play detective. He thought about his friend Kenneth Gresser. It had been a while since they had grabbed a beer and sent a communique to his friend Ken who lived a few blocks down the street. He didn't answer.

Max sighed. He thought of Lydia again and all the work they both had done together. All their travels are for the cause of science. He grabbed a banana and started to eat it as a snack. Throwing the banana peel on the ground, he returned to the bathroom to look in the mirror. He looked through his papers of Ken. Even though Ken was on Mars doing his work, there was still more on Earth. *What was he doing there?*

In the stillness of the east side of the Mars colony, flowing water could be heard. Ken stood in front of a computer image of a dinosaur. Mars housed the headquarters for the scientific work of Ken, Lydia, and Max. Turning in circles in his chair he looked at the latest data. There was nothing out there. In his office, Ken threw some darts at a star map and pondered the color of an *Amaragsaurus*. It had been a while since he had done some observing. Telescopes monitored signals from space on Mars. There had not been any clues. Everything had been quiet. He still knew Lydia and Max, and he was on to something. It was something groundbreaking. Ken held the key to the outside world with his agenda.

He studied all the latest paleontological, geological, and archaeological evidence they could find. It all pointed out that they would be back. The dinosaur will be back someday. But what did that mean now that humanity was among the stars?

Ken continued to think. He still needed funding before the project's exposition later that year. Several corporations were interested in funding. More were expected in the future. A dust storm was forecasted on Mars near the colony. He needed to get to the other side of the colony. His suit was on the other side of his domicile. All this sitting around made him want to work on his scientific endeavors.

He could not help thinking about Lydia. She was beautiful and brilliant. Wandering over to his desk he took a seat to look through some data. There was still nothing. It was leading nowhere. He thought of different routes the project could take. It could expand to all seven continents on Earth, and even the Moon, and Mars. And all the rest of the inhabited or once-inhabited celestial bodies of the solar system.

Looking out the window, he sat gazing at the red planet's terrain. He was the current head of the project. The duties passed between the three of them. Finally, he decided. He would extend the project to all the known sciences.

What would these sciences contribute to? The Fermi Paradox was one of the most interesting paradoxes Ken had encountered. Why are we alone in the universe? Humanity continued to push space exploration despite the fact. He would use some more resources to expand research on the Fermi Paradox.

A chill went through his home on the Mars colony.

"Computer, please, adjust environmental settings," said Ken.

"Acknowledged," said the Mars colony computer. The computer's name was Levi. It was almost self-aware. In just a few more years, it would be capable of reaching a human level of intelligence. Ken went to his desk and wrote down a note. He would need funding to put Levi to work on the project as well. Thinking for a moment, Ken grabbed his writing pad. He took some notes. He needed Levi to calculate some new chemistry problems. *Could there be residual elements from the time they were here?* he thought. A late night at the lab would satisfy some of his questions.

He grabbed his jacket. The environmental systems were starting to experience imbalances because of the dust storm. Maybe tonight was the night they would make their breakthrough. His home was on the upper levels of the colony and the labs were on the lower decks on the other side. The labs were by telescopes. Inserting his badge to open the door, he could hear the howl of the wind.

He walked into the room and the labs immediately powered on and Ken could see which data it displayed. It was about an hour or two in the labs and he went through the full gamut of the sciences from chemistry, biology, and physics to anthropology.

When he was looking at some chemical signals from the latest archeological from Earth and the latest geologic findings from Mars, he heard Levi turn on in the lab.

"Sirzz," he said, "a signal is being detected in the telescope room," said Levi.

"Record it," said Ken.

"Recording," said Levi.

Ken swirled in his chair to look at what the data the telescope room was pumping from the computers. It was indeed a signal. From just outside the solar system. What else could he find?

"Levid," said Ken. "Program the telescope to detect moving objects in the vicinity where the signal was detected. Levi adjusted the telescope. He looked at the computers and what he saw astounded him.

CHAPTER IV

Lydia looked at all the recent data on her plane flight to Seattle. She could not believe it. *They have been here* she thought. She looked out the window. The clouds passed by gently. She had not seen Max for a while. She had taken all the projects needed, but was it too many? Their relationship had come under strain. *Now that they have found their answer, what would happen next?*

The plane safely touched down in Seattle. Lydia awoke from a nap and then left to get her luggage. She walked outside and quickly flagged down a taxi. She got in as the traffic increased. There was light rain and the sound of the rain against the windows of the taxi was comforting. She still hurts from the breakup between her and Max. The work must continue though.

The taxi was driving to Max's house. She put on a jacket inside the car since it was cold. She never liked paying for a taxi or even tipping a taxi driver. As the taxi found its destination, she decided to go against what she usually does. Lydia got out of the taxi and the taxi driver quickly got her luggage.

Max's house was stunning. It was a mansion. One of those new types that architects were getting built. She made her way up to the front door. The doorbell rang throughout the house as she pressed it. A dog barked. It was Gus, Max's beagle. Max opened the door.

Lydia put on a pleasant smile but decided to throw her arms around him.

"It's been forever," she said.

"When was the last time?" he said.

"Oh, over three years ago," said Lydia.

"Come inside, I made dinner," said Max.

Lydia grabbed Max's arm and he led her into his home. Max covered Lydia's eyes as she headed into the dining room. Gus barked at Lydia.

"Let me see," she said.

"Ok," Max said.

Lydia quickly looked around the dining room. Everything was set perfectly in place. She could smell the aroma and she wondered how long it took Max to make it.

"Max you shouldn't have," said Lydia.

Max had not seen Lydia's beauty in a long time. They both sat down at the table. Looking into Lydia's eyes, Max poured some wine.

"So, how have you been? How has your work gone," said Max.

"Cutting to the chase, Max?" said Lydia.

"Yes, I am. You looked very pleasant coming from the airport."

"Well, Max we should contact Ken. I think this discovery means more than drinking wine. What does it mean?" said Lydi,. "All the data says they left a calling card. Humanity's advances in the sciences have finally let us say they were here and little more about them," said Lydia.

"So, you think this is going beyond 65 million years ago or something," said Max.

"That's what all the data is pointing to. I'm saying they established their civilization that was wiped away over time," said Lydia.

Max wiped his mouth with his napkin. Then, he poured some wine into Lydia's wine glass. He cleared his throat. He looked out the window at the shimmering lights of the city.

"What does this mean about the Mars mission and colony?" demanded Max.

"I have not heard back from Ken," said Lydia.

A sense of unease filled the space between them. Ken was still on Mars, and they were both hoping good news would come from his research. Lydia toyed with her hair while Max ate the last of his dinner.

CHAPTER V

It took 130 million years for dinosaurs to evolve. They established a lengthy reign throughout the world. *What did those millions of years mean?* thought Ken. He looked at the data and the telescopes scouted the Martian sky.

Ken slept on a cot ever since that night next to the computers. He scoured through his notes every day. The data also matches up with the notes. He needed one more signal to confirm that they were out there, and they left Earth.

Ken was asleep when he started to hear the ping of the computer signifying a moving object in outer space. He grabbed a pen and paper and did some calculations. It was moving to the Mars colony. The moving object would either hit Mars, pass by, or obtain an orbit around the planet. Moving quickly through the lab he sent a message to Lydia and Max. Calculating again Ken made the prediction the object would get into an orbit around Mars.

The calculations and the data said you could see it from the colony. It would shine brightly. What kind of object was it?

Ken went outside to the atriums and looked up at the night sky. The moving object looked like a blazing comet. *How could that be?* thought Ken. Going back inside he went to some of his instruments to capture a picture. At first, the image was blurry then it became finer. It looked like the object was breaking up in the sky and revealing something else. Barely believing what he was seeing he sent a message to Max and Lydia.

VI

Max flipped open his phone. Ken left a message. He rolled over to find Lydia sleeping next to him. There was a note on the phone signaling it was urgent. He gathered himself together wiping his groggy eyes and sat up in bed. Then, he made his way over to the computer.

Opening the message Max read it. Excitement rose through him. The message from Ken said he at first found some interstellar object and it turned out to be a spaceship upon closer inspection. As soon as he finished reading the message, Max began to plot on a star map. *Where did they come from?* he said.

He thought of all the mythic tales of dragons and other mythical beasts that could be confirmed as once living. The mythic beasts on Earth always came from the sky. The dragons and beasts meant something. The scientific community had spent years running tests, doing explorations, and working on Mars to confirm dinosaurs were once on Earth and Mars.

This spaceship was humanity's first encounter. Certain segments of humanity are frightened of what this endeavor has discovered; others are intrigued. Countless questions filled Max's head. *Were they friendly?* he thought. Max sent a message back to Ken. Lydia woke up and went downstairs to cook some breakfast.

Max smelled like she was cooking eggs. He went downstairs and into the kitchen. Lydia looked up from the stove. "What's going on?" she said.

"We got a message from Ken. He found something great out there in space. Something that will change everything like your scientific findings have done," said Max.

"It must be good," quipped Lydia.

"He said he found a spaceship!" said Max.

"No, you are crazy. I said dinosaurs once had a civilization not that they outdid us in thinking ability."

"Is that what these findings mean?" touted Max.

"Well from a simple calculation, what a million years could do to a complex brain. I would say 'Yes,' said Lydia.

"Do you think they are friendly," said Max.

"Now that, sir," chimed Lydia, "We will have to find out for ourselves.

VII

Ken looked at some of the ancient monsters on the viewscreen in the lab. He liked the monster from Japan. It was called the *Yamata no Orochi*. It had eight heads. The Aztec story of a dragon named *Cipactli* was also interesting. Unlike the dinosaurs, these beings had supernatural powers. What Ken was seeing in the sky above Mars was supernatural, almost divine. Curiosity stirred in him. The computer let out a ping. Ken received a message from Max.

The message rMax and Lydia would travel to Mars from Earth. *They must have good research data*, thought Ken. Ken decided to go to the other end of the colony where shuttles were located. He must see this object himself. He must make it past security though.

He went into his office and gathered his things. To trick the security system, he displayed a hologram on the other side of the colony. It was a hologram of someone burglarizing the colony. He ran and made it to the launch pad for the shuttle. He boarded the shuttle and inputted coordinates for intercepting the object.

The Martian night sky flew past Ken. Before he knew it, he was in space. The hull of the ship was covered with ice like a comet. He spotted what looked like a landing area. A scan of the ship showed no life signs. The shuttle got close to the ship and it landed successfully. Ken let out a sigh of relief. He took another scan of the ship and the scan showed a slightly different concentration of gases from the environment of Earth. Ken grabbed a mask.

The spaceship was quiet. He pressed a control panel to put him onto the deck outside the landing area. A thick fog was everywhere on the deck and the lighting was low. He kept moving on the deck and after a while, he grabbed a flashlight. Sweat was coming from his brow. Whatever was here living liked it a bit warm. Suddenly, he heard footsteps.

His body shook in fright. A wet substance fell onto his mask from behind him. Before he knew it though, he passed out from fear.

VIII

Max looked at the blackness of space while approaching Mars. Lydia flipped through the rest of her notes about the research. It had been a while since they heard from Ken. The weather on Mars was getting better.

The spaceship landed on the outskirts of the Martian colony. Before Max and Lydia got off the ship, Max messaged Ken. They walked through the space dock and walked onto the colony. There were plenty of people milling about at the space dock and memories of past trips to Mars flashed before him. He was earnest to see the main area of the colony. Lydia grabbed Max's arm.

"Time to go," she said.

Max was slightly perturbed by Lydia commanding the lead, but he thought she would let her take the lead this time. They finally reached the main area of the colony. Max looked for a message on his scientific instrument from Ken. There was nothing.

"Time to head to the labs and telescopes," said Ken.

Lydia smiled and then Ken took the lead to the laboratories. Lydia had not seen Ken in a while, so she was thrilled to see him. She wondered if Max and him would cooperate like they have before to get the work accomplished.

"I'm excited to see Ken's latest work and why we are here," said Lydia.

"Yes, so am I," said Max.

Max thought about what else could be in store. He still felt a sense of unease about Ken's discovery. *What did it mean to work of Lydia and him? he thought.* They arrived at the laboratories.

Lydia and Max quickly looked around the laboratory. Their security cards had let them into with ease. There were signs of a rushed exit. They looked at the computers and saw images of what looked like a comet.

"This is fascinating," said Lydia. "But why would he leave."

"He left because of the implications. We would have to reconsider our theory of evolution," said Max.

"Do you think it's safe up there," said Lydia, "It must be cold so whatever is there is either the Yeti or not what we are looking for."

Max looked around further in the laboratory. He found some old textbooks and more images. Some showed mythical monsters.

"I am guessing Ken was working on a clue," said Max. Max searched through the texts of the manuscripts and finally found some notes of Ken. It was all speculation about mythical beasts from the sky.

"I guess he just took a leap of faith and went up there," said Max.

Suddenly there was a ping from the computer. Lydia brought Max over to the computer. They both stared in relief. It was Ken, but it was a distress signal.

"He's up there on the ship," said Max. "Whatever is up there is not very friendly.

We need to go up there and get him back."

CHAPTER IX

Max and Lydia grabbed their research materials, put on a spacesuit, and ran to the shuttle area. They looked around the shuttle landing and take-off area for any suspicious activity. Max inputted the coordinates for the comet-turned-spaceship.

Before they knew it, Max landed the shuttle on the ship. They needed to get inside the ship. Before they searched anymore, they happened to spot Ken's shuttle. It was at some kind of space dock. They both scanned the area to see what kind of clues they could find. Their instruments showed Ken took a scan of the ship and its environmental system before the signal pinged and then faded. They walked onto the ship.

They found Ken's mask on the floor of one of the decks close to the space dock. The spacesuits detected a higher pulse rate from Max and Lydia. Sweat started to drip from their foreheads.

"Don't take off your mask," said Max. "The atmosphere is too different."

"Who would breathe this stuff?" said Lydia

"Something very big and mean," said Max.

They wandered their way to another deck and there was what looked like a control panel. Max brought one of his instruments and managed to get a schematic of the ship. In the darkness of the ship they heard strange noises. *Was it an animal?*

"I found the main area of the ship—the commanding deck," said Max.

"Max come look at this," said Lydia. She had wandered into a room that had been sealed off from the rest of the ship. Max and Lydia started to breathe heavily.

Bringing out his flashlight, Max started to process what he was seeing. They were murals. *Some kind of map, maybe a star map?* he thought. Max took out one of his instruments and scanned the murals and other archeological findings. The murals and everything all pointed to Ken's theory in his notes. People of Earth had met these creatures before in their hsitory. A noise was heard from behind Ken and Lydia.

They both turned around and beamed their flashlights at the direction of the noise. To their surprise, something was looking back at them. It was a *Velociraptor*; an acutal *Velociraptor*. It screeched at them, and both Max and Lydia looked at each other.

"Run!" said Max, as he turned around, he shot at the *Velociraptor* stunning it. They both continued to run in the direction of another door across the room filled with murals. Finding the safety of another deck they closed and sealed the door behind them.

"I am worried about Ken," said Lydia. "It's true. I can't believe it. It's all true. This will revolutionize everything. We knew they could fly but we did not know they flew in space."

"Yes, you are right. But who is piloting this thing is the question," said Max.

Walking to the command area, they spotted another room. Ken scanned the area. Frost appeared on their face masks.

"These look like sleep chambers. One is open and the occupant is gone and another one. The rest are still in working order," said Max.

Lydia stared at the sleep chambers and did a scan. She wiped away some frost from the head area of the sleep chamber. What was there took her breath away.

"They're humanoid and reptilian," said Lydia. She scanned the bodies of the sleeping reptiles, getting as much data as possible. Scanning the two opened sleep chambers puddles of ooze. Upon close inspection, she saw signs and symbols that indicated a language.

"Damn, I wish I had studied linguistics," said Lydia. The scanner began deciphering the script. The panel with the script started to glow. Light pulsated through the chambers.

"We better get going and find Ken," said Lydia. "I found this mask of his on the floor." Max looked at his scanner again and it started to put up a human life sign. The scan intensified and came back positive as Ken.

"He is at the command center. And there are not any obstacles in our way there," said Max.

CHAPTER X

Max and Lydia held their stun guns in position. They arrived at the command center. In the center was a chair. They scoped out the rest of the command center. When they turned around the chair, it was Ken unconscious. Max automatically checked his pulse. He was alive.

"Oh my God, what do you think happened?" said Lydia.

"I do not know. But I do not want to meet it," said Max picking up Ken by the shoulders.

Ken let out a groan.

"He's waking up" clamored Lydia.

Max sat him against a wall. "Who did this to you?" questioned Max.

"Therapod," said Ken. "It was a therapod humanoid," whimpered Ken. "There's also a *Velociraptor*. Just leave. Just go. It's a trap. Please."

"I'm not leaving you" comforted Max. Lydia gave Ken a sedative. The lights flickered on and off in the command center.

Before Max could grab Ken again a form materialized before him. It was a humanoid reptilian. Its skin was a lush green speckled with brown and it had eyes on the sides of its head. Nostrils were slits on his protruding nose and face. It started to hiss at Lydia and Ken.

"Max!" said Lydia.

"Don't move," said Max.

The reptilian became aggressive and let out a screech. Max waited for the alien to make a move toward him. It stood there like it was reading his mind. *Did it understand the situation it was in?* thought Max. Ken continued to groan.

"I'm putting the translator on," said Lydia filled with dread.

"Who are you?" said Max.

The translator processed Max's word and the alien seemed more attentive. It blinked then. It then, said something. It was a combination of clicks, grunts, and screeches. Max and Lydia winced at the sounds.

"I'm Zonit," said the alien. The alien blinked with his slitty eyes. His breathing was heavy and noticeable. Zonit looked like he was in some kind of uniform.

"Are you with others?" inquired Max.

"Yes, there are others. But only one managed to awake from their sleep chamber safely," said Zonit.

"How long have you been asleep?" said Max.

"It has been some time since we were in the sleep chamber. And we require attention," said Zonit.

Max looked at the alien closely. It was almost like he was reading his mind. He started to quiver. His mind sensed an intruder.

CHAPTER XI

The alien seemed calmer, but Max and Lydia did not have their answers yet. The three all stood unwavering until Zonit broke the silence. His nostrils flared as he began to articulate his alien language.

"What you want I may not be able to give? said Zonit.

"Where is this ship going?" pursued Max.

"It's going to the planet named Earth in our revered history. A planet we have been on too long ago," said Zonit.

"What do you want with it?" questioned Lydia.

"Well, we want everything it's our home," said Zonit.

"So, you're from Earth. You look like some kind of dinosaur in human form," said Max. "Do you expect me to believe this?"

"Max don't screw with this research and quit the attitude," instructed Lydia.

"Ken is beginning to come around," said Lydia. "Ken it's me Lydia."

"They are in our mythology Lydia and Max. Everything was going great until he said they called Earth their home and wanted us gone."

"It's been some time since we made it back to Earth," stated Zonit.

"What kind of ship is this?" inquired Max.

"It is sleeper and arc ship. There are other unevolved kinds of me on this ship which you call the dinosaur. Your friend met one and did the right thing by running from it. That's how he met me," said Zonit.

"He needs medical attention," said Max.

The ship started to produce metal sounds of the hull starting to buckle. Zonit went over to the console. Max noted how the dinosaur's hands evolved. Lydia was processing all the linguistic information she could through the translator.

"The ship is losing its cover," said Zonit, "We're being pulled to close to Mars."

Ken opened his eyes he saw Max and Lydia in front of him. He knew what the alien wanted, Earth. They intended to drive humanity into slavery or extinction. Screeches and bellows filled the command center.

"Why would you want to harm the people of Earth? Has your species gone insane? You are in our mythology. Once aliens were our teacher," said Max.

"Truth is harder to comprehend," touted Zonit. "To end this stalemate, I suggest an exchange. Or you may turn into food."

"What kind of exchange?" said Lydia

"You have come a long way humans. But my kind needs technology to prevent us from dying and devolving," said Zonit. "I'm not asking for much. Just an exchange of technology."

Ken stood between Max and Lydia. Lydia gave him a stun gun, but she motioned to set it to kill. Max watched as the alien screeched and clicked over a device. The screeching and bellows became louder. Zonit spoke to the three of them.

"Hand over the information about your latest technology," said Zonit, "And my unevolved cousins will spare your life."

"We can only give you what we have," said Max.

Zonit looked like he was hiding something. The consoles of the command center were coming more online. Max and Lydia completed an information download and put it on a device. Lydia noticed blood coming from Max's ears.

"Max, are you alright? You're bleeding," said Lydia in a concerned voice.

"I feel...I feel...I've never felt like this before. It feels like someone is inside my mind," said Max.

"Precisely," stated Zonit, "You have experienced loss, human. Just like some of my species. Children without a mother and father. Famine, disease, and war are everywhere. This has motivated you in your search. Some say it was a wild goose chase. It turns out they were wrong."

"How do you know that I've experienced loss? Please be more specific," said Max.

"I read your mind. We all have experienced loss. You lost your parents when you were young. As a consequence, you searched for something. to silence your mind. Your research soothed your mind, but it started to hurt your soul. Yes, I believe in a soul," cooed Zonit.

Max looked like he did not know what to say. He decided to inquire more as he handed over the information containing a technology exchange. He furrowed his brow and considered what he was about to say.

"My parents, can you bring them back from the afterlife? Your biological technology is more advanced," said Max. Pounding on metal was heard at the command center's door. The other aliens—dinosaurs—were here. Ken, Lydia, and Max started to panic.

CHAPTER XII

"You three must go," said Zonit.

"But Earth! Why do you want to go there? We are innocent," yelled Ken.

The ship jolted and Zonit and three of them were thrown to the floor. A schematic popped on a schematic. Max studied it.

"The ship! The course of the ship is now Earth," said Max. "You lied!"

Zonit opened his hands to signal he meant no harm. Max. Ken, and Lydia made their way over to the other side of the command center they went through a door. They reached the shuttle.

"The systems are down," said Max.

"We don't need our masks," instructed Ken.

"Are you sure?" said Lydia.

Max was using one of his instruments to try to get the shuttles back online. His hands were shaking, and he breathed heavily. Ken and Lydia watched earnestly for an answer from Max.

Suddenly, the consoles began to pulse with power and light. Sparks flew into the air. The hree covered their faces. Blood started to run from their ears. And soon they passed out into a deep sleep.

When they woke up, they were still in the shuttle. Max, Lydia, and Ken tried to shake up the woozy effect of suddenly going unconscious. Max punched the chair in frustration.

"Where are we? said Ken.

"We are still on the ship," said Max.

Max looked at the coordinates. The ship was now orbiting Earth. *We need to get to Zonit,* he thought. Screeching and bellows could still be heard throughout the ship.

"Have your stun guns ready and set to kill," said Max.

They made their way back to the command center. Zonit was standing at the front of it. Another alien was standing next to him.

Zonit touched the console. Lydia, Max, and Ken stared in amazement at what happened. A beam of light was sent down to the Earth. The area was populated. It was Istanbul,

Turkey. Images flew past Zonit . They were images of people running and screaming.

"Zonit! What is going on?" said Max.

"Your kind will soon start to go through extinction on this planet," said Zonit.

The other reptilian alien seemed female. She had an ardent gaze at the events happening on Earth. Small therapod dinosaurs were at her feet.

"This is Thera," said Zonit.

"She is my companion. She is my mate who you would call a wife," Zonit said in a gleeful voice.

"Soon the rest of our evolve kind will arrive here," clicked Thera "To help with the process.

"What process?" questioned Lydia.

"Take a look for yourself," said Thera.

Dust was everywhere at the site the beam touched. Forms started to emerge from the chaos. To Ken, Lydia, and Max's disbelief. Dinosaurs were emerging from the ground. Bones with flesh materializing on them.

"Our greatest achievement," said Zonit in a triumphant tone.

"We bring life back from the dead," said Thera.

"O my god," said Lydia, "They're alive. But all the research pointed out that they pointed to an actual civilization. There's hope for our two species. Your technology can help save the problems on Earth."

Ken looked at Lydia. Myths were now fact. The myths were living and breathing. The theories of science turned on their heads.

"We built a civilization in a million years," said Zonit. "We reached our apogee. Then the asteroid strike happened."

Lydia and Ken were waiting for orders from Max. They must shut down the resurrection beam. Max looked confused.

"You read my mind Zonit. Can you bring them back?" said Max.

Zonit turned round a looked at them. He snarled. Thera did the same.

"I would prefer to turn you into food," said Zonit.

He pressed the command center console panel and the doors of the center opened. A menacing therapod dinosaur Max. The therapod screeched making Max, Lydia, and Ken wince. Thera and Zonit walked away and exited the command center.

The therapod dinosaur ran towards the three of them. It was getting ready to strike. Its menacing claws slicing the air. They opened fire on the dinosaur. It ducked and finally jumped into the air. And, the creature struck Ken. Ken fell back and blood spewed forth from his chest. The dinosaur killed him.

Lydia opened fire and she struck the dinosaur's head. It screamed in pain. And it landed on the command center's floor with a thud.

"No, no, no, Ken. Don't die," Lydia said as she held Ken. She started to sob. Max was frantic. He must try to get to the alien's technology. They knew how to resurrect life. Somehow Max managed to open a file from the console. Zonit downloaded his consciousness to the ship. Memories of his parents were there.

Lydia was crying over Ken. Max believed he was dead, but there was no time to know. One of his instruments beeped. Someone was approaching. Max got up and ran towards the door. He made it out of the command center and headed towards the shuttle.

Max checked all the shuttle systems. They were operational. He plugged in some coordinates. The mechanics of the shuttle whirled, and the landing dock was opening to space. Guiding the shuttle out Max looked down to see a resurrection beam. This one was in the territory of the former United States of America. It was Oregon. His parents were buried in Oregon by a cabin they used to have when they were living. It took a while for the shuttle to reach a landing spot, but eventually, Max guided it successfully.

Max stepped out of the shuttle. The light from the resurrection beam was everywhere. Two forms began to appear. Max began to cry.

"Mom! Dad," he said.

When the forms materialized, it was them. His mom and dad reached out to him. Max buried his head in his father's chest and sobbed.

"I miss you guys so much more than the world could ever know!" exclaimed Max.

Max's mom wiped away some of Zach's tears. Dad's father did the same. A blue hue was everywhere. Max held the hands of his mother and father. He could not believe it.

The light from the resurrection beam started to intensify and then fade. Max's parents looked like a mere illusion at times. He started to touch them again. His hands only started to go through the air.

"No, no, don't go," said Max to his parents.

They flickered back and forth materializing here and there. They disappeared. Max heard another shuttle behind him. It was Lydia.

"Max! Ken is dead," said Lydia.

"The resurrection beam will help him," said Max.

Ken's eyes began to dart back and forth. One of Ken's instruments detected brain activity. Before Max's eyes, the wound on Ken's chest began to heal. His eyes started to open. Lydia started to cry in elation.

"It worked," she said. "I thought I lost you," said Lydia.

Ken breathed a sigh of relief. He absorbed his surroundings. His breathing became normal.

"We're back home," said Ken.

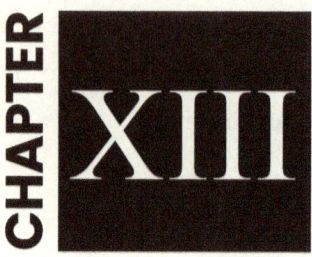

CHAPTER XIII

Max went back to the shuttle. He looked and read the latest news. Zonit's ship was emitting plenty of resurrection beams. There were plenty of dinosaurs making havoc now. They were in London, Paris, Tokyo, Beijing, and Rio de Janeiro.

Max motioned to Lydia and Ken. They were holding each other. He had never thought there was a romance between them.

"Get in the shuttle," said Max.

They obeyed. Max glared at them. He had forgotten his pursuit of Lydia. It almost did not matter to him since he got to see his parents to him. There was hope he could have them back.

Taking a seat in the pilot's chair, Max plotted a course for Madrid, Spain. There are some interesting dinosaurs

Max wanted to see. The shuttle lifted from the ground and took flight.

From the air, all three could see the dinosaurs walking on the land of Spain. Some were gigantic new sauropod dinosaurs and they saw a couple of pterosaurs close to the shuttle. Max inputted some commands on the shuttle's console and began to scan the news.

"Global news is saying world leaders are considering the resurrection beam an attack by a hostile force," said Max.

"How do we make it back to the ship?" said Lydia.

"Luck," chuckled Max.

Max guided the shuttle back to the ship. When everyone was on board, he accessed the consoles from Zonit's ship. The ship jolted and the console signaled trouble.

The consoles read that Zonit's ship was taking hits from Earth. The ship recalibrated its systems. It had shields. Once Max activated them the weapons were deflected from the ship.

Max, Lydia, and Ken look around the command center. They had seen a lot. And it only perked their interest.

"Where's Zonit?," said Lydia.

"We need to make it back to the sleep chambers?" said Ken.

"Agreed," concurred Max.

Before they left the command center, they scanned the decks they were about to enter. No life signs were detected.

The screeching and bellowing of dinosaurs was still faint. They entered the room with the sleep chambers. Zonit stood alone over one of the sleep chambers.

"Zonit, we need your help! We need you to convince leaders back on Earth you are not a threat," said Max.

Zonit had his hands placed in a sleep chamber.

"She was the only one for me," said Zonit. Lydia and Ken looked at each other. What looked like tears gathered beneath Zonit's eyes.

"What happened?" said Lydia.

"I had to put her back in the sleep chamber. She contracted a virus," said Zonit.

"I'm sorry," said Max.

Lydia and Ken looked at Zonit. His breath grew heavy. He squinted, the slits of his eyes growing smaller.

"I can see you know what humans know as love," said Zonit.

Max did not care about Lydia and Ken. He now only cared about the world leaders and getting his parents back to the world of the living. Zonit walked to Max and placed a hand on Max. Zonit began to read Max's mind. He began to know where Max's heart was placed.

"What will happen to you Zonit? What will happen to the ship?" insisted Max.

"More of my kind will arrive. Negotiations will have to take place now. Science has been on turned its head in the eyes of humanity. My kind are civilized they know what to do," said Zonit.

Max placed his hand on Zonit's shoulder and smiled in return. Zonit looked sad. Max knew why. He found his home, Earth.

"When our bones settle, the earth will be quiet again," said Zonit. "It's a saying from our religion."

"What about your cousins on Earth, the unevolved ones," said Max.

"They'll make it. I've already placed some satellites in orbit to monitor them. Evolution will take its course again," said Zonit.

"Can you bring back Max's parents back for sure?" inquired Ken.

Max looked back at Lydia and Ken. They looked happy together. Losing was hard, but knowing they had started a relationship was even harder.

"We'll go back to the Earth's surface, Max," said Lydia.

"May the Earth sit in stillness when your bones settle, Max" said Zonit.

There was so much more to these space-faring dinosaurs, thought Max. He had waited his whole life to see where science had taken humanity. He welcomed Zonit's saying which in human terms would ring as a prayer. Max walked over to Lydia and Ken. Zonit gathered himself. He stepped in a sleep chamber and laid back in it. It began to close and a whisp of air was heard.

"We need to go before the ship leaves orbit," said Lydia.

"Agreed," said Max and Ken.

They made their way over to the shuttle area. A blue, green, and brown Earth lay below them. They guided the shuttle successfully. They were headed for Seattle, Washington. All three listened to the latest news broadcasts of dinosaurs now walking the Earth again. When they finally reached, Seattle, Washington all three were asleep. Autopilot was on to guide the shuttle. An alarm went off on the computer inside the computer. All three of them woke up and looked out the window. They made it back home. Lydia and Ken got out of the shuttle. Max followed. The air of the Pacific Northwest filled their lungs.

"Well, it's been great Ken," said Max.

"Yeah," said Ken. "You saved my life."

"No problem. I was once a lifeguard. It comes with the territory," said Max.

Lydia remained quiet but her eyes indicated she was sincere. Max would miss her, but his ambition said he would be fine. They walked to the nearest public transportation station. Max went to his pocket. He looked down at his hand and studied a picture of his parents. He had made it back home.

www.ingramcontent.com/pod-product-compliance
Lightning Source LLC
Chambersburg PA
CBHW020236120726
47903CB00008B/2698